EPSILON
A YELLOWSTONE WOLF STORY

TED RECHLIN

RIVERBEND
PUBLISHING

Epsilon: A Yellowstone Wolf Story
Copyright © 2013 by Ted Rechlin

Published by Riverbend Publishing, Helena, Montana

ISBN 13: 978-1-60639-064-1

Printed in the USA

3 4 5 6 VP 25 24 23 22 21

Cover design by Ted Rechlin

Riverbend Publishing
P.O. Box 5833
Helena, MT 59604
1-866-787-2363
www.riverbendpublishing.com

AND THIS VALLEY- THE LAMAR VALLEY- IS THEIR HOME, THEIR TERRITORY.

SEE, IF YOU'RE A WOLF, THERE'S A REASON YOU WANT TO LIVE IN THE LAMAR VALLEY.

SO JUST LIKE THAT, THE THREE YOUNG WOLVES WENT FROM HEIRS TO THE THRONE TO OUT IN THE COLD.

EPSILON.

BROTHER, BETA.

AND SISTER, THETA.

DRIVEN FROM THEIR HOME TERRITORY, ON THEIR OWN IN ANOTHER PART OF YELLOWSTONE. THEY HAD BECOME THE EXILE PACK.

THE EXILE PACK DIDN'T HAVE THE SMOOTHEST OF STARTS.

CLEARLY, LEARNING HOW TO HUNT WAS GOING TO TAKE SOME TIME.

THEY JUST HAD TO FIND THEIR SPECIALTY.

THEY HAD TO LEARN TO WORK AS A TEAM, TO HUNT LIKE A PACK OF WOLVES.

EPSILON KNEW THAT SQUIRRELS ARE GREAT, BUT WHEN YOU'RE A HUNGRY AND GROWING WOLF...

...WITH TWO HUNGRY AND GROWING WOLF SIBLINGS...

...YOU NEED TO GRADUATE TO BIGGER AND BETTER THINGS.

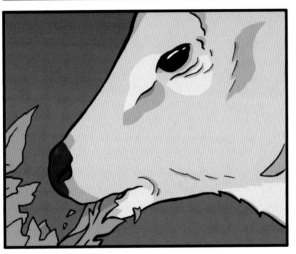

AND, AS TIME WENT ON, THAT'S WHAT THEY DID.

EPSILON KNEW HE WAS TOO CLOSE TO THE LAMAR VALLEY. BUT SNOW IN YELLOWSTONE HAS A WAY OF MAKING YOU CHANGE YOUR PLANS.

AWOOOOOOOOOOOOOOO

THE THUNDERERS.

OLDER WOLVES. STRONGER. NOT BOTHERED BY A LITTLE SNOW.

RRRR...

YIP!

WOOOOOOOO

THERE'S SOMETHING THAT HAPPENS TO WOLVES WHEN THEY TURN TWO YEARS OLD.

BETA WAS FIRST TO GO OFF ON HIS OWN.

AND IT WAS DURING THE EXILES' SECOND WINTER THAT IT HAPPENED TO THEM.

NOT LONG AFTER, EPSILON AND THETA SEPARATED AS WELL. THEY WERE EACH LOOKING FOR MATES.

THAT WINTER, A WOLF CALLED ACCALIA SPLIT FROM HER PACK TOO.

WHERE SHE CAME FROM, EPSILON DIDN'T KNOW.

WHAT HE DID KNOW WAS THAT SHE WAS ALONE, LIKE HIM, AND HE WAS HAPPY TO FIND HER.

AND THE REST, AS THEY SAY. . .

ADULT WOLVES LOVE PUPS.

AND EPSILON, ACCALIA, AND BETA WERE NO EXCEPTIONS.

BUT PUPS GOTTA EAT.

WOLF PUPS GROW FAST AND EPSILON AND BETA WERE PRETTY BUSY GETTING FOOD FOR ACCALIA AND SIX VERY HUNGRY LITTLE MOUTHS.

NOT THAT ACCALIA HAD MUCH FREE TIME OF HER OWN.

WITH BETA ALWAYS THERE TO BE COUNTED ON, EPSILON AND ACCALIA HAD BECOME THE ALPHA WOLVES OF A PACK TWELVE STRONG.

THE THUNDERER PACK.

WOOOOOOOOOO

EPSILON KNOWS THAT THEY ARE A STRONG PACK.

AAWOOOO

BUT TIMES HAVE CHANGED, AND HE CAN HEAR IT IN THEIR VOICES.

THEY'RE NOT WHAT THEY USED TO BE.

THIS IS NOBLE TERRITORY.

AND NOBLE PACK HAS RETURNED TO TAKE IT BACK.

THE THUNDERER'S ALPHA MALE WOLF.

HE'S EPSILON'S TARGET.

BEAT A PACK'S ALPHA WOLVES AND BREAK THE PACK. EPSILON KNOW THIS.

AND...

IT'S A COOL MORNING IN YELLOWSTONE AND AN OLD BLACK WOLF NAMED EPSILON HAS BROUGHT HIS PACK— HIS FAMILY— HOME. NO LONGER EXILES, ONCE AGAIN THEY ARE THE NOBLE PACK.

ABOUT THE ARTIST/AUTHOR

Ted Rechlin has worked professionally in picture book illustration, comic book art, trading cards, graphic design, and tattoo design.

Most of Ted's time is spent at the drawing board, working on illustration projects, or teaching his craft to aspiring artists.

When Ted's not working at his Bozeman, Montana, home, he can usually be found hiking the Yellowstone backcountry.

For more information on Ted's art, teaching, and appearances, visit www.tedrechlinart.com.

ALSO BY TED RECHLIN

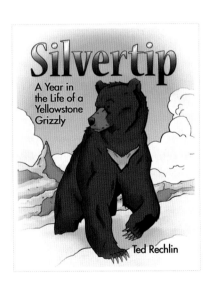